Gon, The Little Fox

Written by Nankichi Niimi • Illustrated by Genjirou Mita

I

This is a story that I heard in my childhood. It was told to me by an old man named Mohei who lived in my village:

There once was a small castle at a place called Nakayama near our village. The lord of Nakayama lived there.

On a mountain not too far from Nakayama, lived a fox called Gon, the Little Fox. Gon was a lonely cub. He lived in a small hole that he had dug in a forest covered with thick ferns.

Both day and night, Gon liked to visit the nearby village just to stir up mischief. He would sneak into the farms and dig up yams. He would set fire to the rapeseed husks that were laid out in the sun to dry. He would snatch up the cayenne peppers hung in the back of a farmer's house. He did all that and much more.

One autumn, it rained and rained for several straight days. Gon sat in his hole, not able to go out because of the rain.

Finally, the rain stopped. He was relieved and crawled out of the hole. The sky was completely clear, and the squeaking voice of a shrike echoed in the air.

Gon strolled to the bank of the stream that ran through the village. He noticed all around him blades of silver grass still shining from the raindrops. Normally, the stream did not have much water in it. But three days of rain had raised the water nearly above its banks. The silver grass and bush clovers that grew on the banks were bent over and buffeted by the yellow muddy water. Gon walked on a muddy path along the side of the stream.

Then, he saw a human doing something in the middle of the stream. Gon hid in the deep part of the grass and quietly snuck up to look.

"It's Hyoju, all right," he thought. Hyoju had his worn-out dark clothes tucked up in order to get waist-high into the water. He was shaking a fish net called *harikiri*, trying to catch some fish. He wore a headband, and a round bush clover leaf was stuck on the side of his face, as if it were a large mole.

After a while, Hyoju picked up the end of the *harikiri* fish net from the water. Inside the bag-like net was a messy mix of roots, leaves, and rotten sticks, but something white was also shining through. These were the bellies of a large eel and minnow. Hyoju pushed the eel and minnow into a basket with the rest of the mess. Then, he closed the fish net and put it into the water again.

Hyoju got out of the water with his basket, but suddenly left it on the bank to run upstream, as if he were looking for something.

Once Hyoju was out of sight, Gon jumped out of the grass and ran up to the basket. He got the urge to cause some trouble. He grabbed the fish out of the basket and tossed them back one by one into the stream below where Hyoju's fish net was placed. Each fish made a splashing sound and then disappeared into the muddy water.

Gon tried to grab the last fish, which was a large eel, but it was too slippery to grab with his paws. He grew impatient and plunged his head into the basket to bite the head of the eel. The eel made a squeaking sound and coiled around Gon's neck. Just at that moment, Hyoju screamed from the distance, "Hey, you, thieving fox!"

The surprised Gon jumped up and tried to shake the eel off and run away. However, the eel was tightly coiled around his neck and would not come off. Gon jumped sideways and ran away as fast as he could. When he got to the alder tree near his hole, he looked back, but did not see Hyoju coming after him. Relieved, Gon finally bit the eel's head off and left the eel on top of some grass leaves outside his hole.

II

About ten days went by. While Gon was passing behind the house of a farmer called Yasuke, he saw Yasuke's wife blackening her teeth in the shadow of a fig tree. She seemed to be preparing herself for a special occasion. When he passed behind the house of Shinbei the blacksmith, his wife was setting her hair.

Gon thought, "Hmm, something seems to be happening in the village."

"What could it be? Is it the fall festival? If it's the fall festival, I should be hearing the sound of drums or flutes. And most importantly, the banners

10

should be raised at the shrine."

Gon continued to walk and ponder this, and before he knew it, he had come to Hyoju's house; it was small and had a red well in the front. There were many people gathered in the run-down house.

Women in formal clothes with towels hanging from their belts were making a fire in the furnace outside. Something was boiling in a large pot.

"Ah, it's a funeral," Gon figured. "Did someone die in Hyoju's family?"

After lunchtime, Gon went ahead to the village cemetery and hid behind the six Buddha statues there. It was a fine day, and in the distance he could see the castle's roof tiles shining in the sun. In the cemetery, red spider lilies were blossoming as if a red carpet were spread over the ground. Then, he heard the sound of a bell in the distance. It was the sign of a funeral party leaving home.

Soon, he started seeing the people wearing white clothes in a funeral procession coming his way. He could hear their voices as they grew closer. The procession came into the cemetery. After the people passed, the red spider lilies were trampled down.

Gon stretched himself up for a better look. He saw Hyoju wearing a white *kamishimo* costume and carrying a funeral tablet in front of his chest. His normally energetic, reddish face seemed somewhat withered today.

"So, it was Hyoju's mama who passed away," Gon thought, pulling his head back down.

12

That night, in his hole, Gon pondered everything that had happened.

"Hyoju's mama must have been sick in bed and said that she would like to eat an eel. So, Hyoju took the *harikiri* fish net out. But I did mischief and stole the eel so that Hyoju couldn't give his mama any to eat. Mama must have died without eating an eel. She must have died thinking, 'I wanted to eat an eel. I wish I could eat an eel.' Oh, I shouldn't have done such mischief."

15

III

Hyoju was rinsing wheat by the red well.
He and his mama had lived by themselves. Now that she had passed away,
he was left all alone.

"Now, Hyoju is all alone just like me," Gon thought, looking at Hyoju
from behind the storage hut.

Gon was about to leave the hut when he heard the sardine peddler's voice
calling in the distance. "Sardines for sale. Fresh sardines here."

Gon ran toward the high-spirited voice.

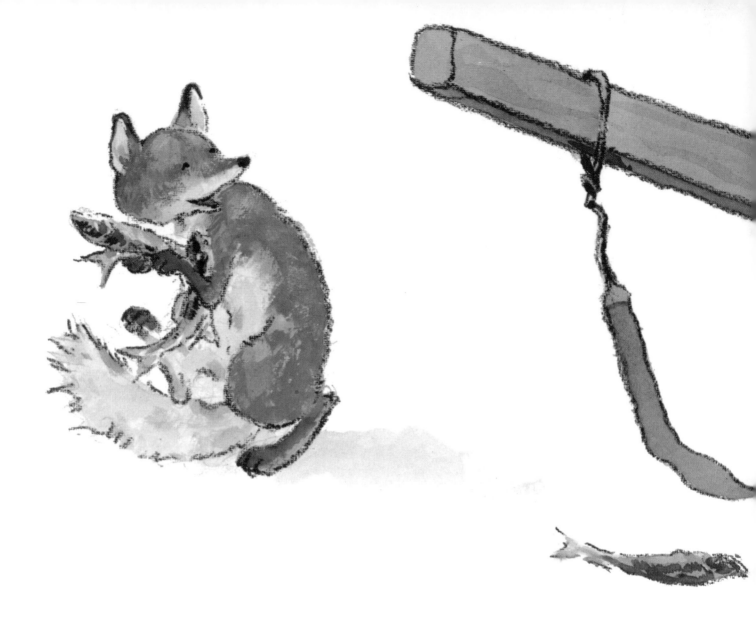

Yasuke's wife called the peddler from the back door of her house, "I'd like some sardines." The sardine peddler stopped his cart, with a basket of sardines on top, by the roadside, grabbed some glittering sardines with both hands, and walked into Yasuke's house.

Gon quickly snatched five or six sardines out of the basket and started running back to where he had come from. He threw the sardines into

Hyoju's house through the back door and quickly ran back to his hole. As he looked back from the top of the hill on the way home, he could see tiny Hyoju in the distance still rinsing wheat by his well.

Gon thought that he had done a good thing by starting to make amends for the eel.

The next day, Gon gathered a lot of chestnuts in the mountains and carried them over to Hyoju's house. When he peeped in from the back door, Hyoju was in the middle of eating lunch. He was holding his bowl in his hand but seemed lost in thought. Gon noticed a strange scratch on Hyoju's cheek. As he wondered what had happened, Hyoju started talking to himself. "Who in the world threw sardines into my house?" he mumbled. "The sardine peddler accused me of stealing from him and gave me a hard time."

Gon thought he had made a mistake by stealing the sardines. He felt sorry for Hyoju for being punched by the sardine peddler and for getting a scratch on his face.

Thinking about this, Gon quietly made his way around the hut, left the chestnuts by the door, and ran home.

The day after, and the day after that, Gon gathered chestnuts and took them to Hyoju's house.

And, the following day, he even left a couple of big mushrooms in addition to the chestnuts.

IV

It was a clear night with a bright moon. Gon wandered off to have some fun. When he had passed below Nakayama castle and had walked a little further on, he heard some people approaching on the narrow path. He could hear them talking. A pine cricket was making its chirping sound.

Gon hid and remained still by the side of the path. The voices were coming closer to him. It was Hyoju and a farmer named Kasuke.

"You know what, Kasuke?" Hyoju said.

"Huh?"

"Some odd things have been happening to me these days."

"Like what?" asked Kasuke.

"Ever since my mama died, somebody, I don't know who, has been giving me things like chestnuts and mushrooms every day."

"Who could it be?" asked Kasuke.

"I don't know," said Hyoju. "Somebody leaves it when I'm not looking."

Gon followed close behind the two men.

"Is that so?" asked Kasuke.

"Oh, yes. If you think I'm lying, you should come see me tomorrow," said Hyoju. "I'll show you the chestnuts."

"Well, strange things can happen," said Kasuke.

The two men kept walking without saying anything more.

Kasuke suddenly turned around. Surprised, Gon froze, making his body small. Kasuke did not see Gon and just kept walking. As they arrived at the house of a farmer called Kichibei, Kasuke and Hyoju went inside. The "bong" sound of a wooden temple block was heard. The window screen was lit from the inside and a shadow of a monk's shaved head was moving on it. Crouching by the well, Gon thought, "They must be having a prayer service." A little later, a group of about three more people entered Kichibei's house.

The voice of prayer chanting could be heard.

V

Gon crouched by the well until the praying ended. Hyoju and Kasuke began to walk home together. Gon followed them, trying to listen to what they were talking about. He crept along, stepping on Hyoju's shadow from time to time.

When they reached the front of the castle, Kasuke started talking.

"You know," said Kasuke, "what you said earlier is probably God's doing."
"What?" Hyoju was surprised and looked at Kasuke's face.

"I've been thinking about it all along. But, I think it is not human. It must be God. He must pity you since you have been left alone and has been blessing you with many things."

"Is that so?" murmured Hyoju in wonder.

"Of course," said Kasuke. "So, you should thank God every day."

"All right," said Hyoju. "I shall thank God every day."

The farmer's talk disappointed Gon.

"I'm the one who has been taking chestnuts and mushrooms to Hyoju. But instead of thanking me, he thanks God. That is unfair to me."

VI

The following day, Gon went again to Hyoju's house to deliver chestnuts. Hyoju was making a rope inside the hut. So, Gon sneaked into the house through the back door.

Hyoju suddenly looked up and saw the fox enter his house. "That must be Gon who stole the eel from me the other day. He's probably back again to do more mischief. All right, then."

Hyoju stood up, carefully took down his flintlock gun that hung in the hut, and loaded it with gunpowder.

Hyoju approached Gon quietly and shot at the fox as he was leaving the house.

32

Gon fell over. Hyoju ran to the fox. As he looked inside the house, he noticed a pile of chestnuts.

"Huh?" Surprised, Hyoju looked down at Gon.

"Gon, was it you? Were you the one who kept bringing me chestnuts?"

Gon, slumped on the ground with his eyes closed, nodded.

The gun dropped from Hyoju's hand. Thin blue smoke was still coming out of the muzzle.

GON, THE LITTLE FOX

Gongitsune by Nankichi Niimi & Genjirou Mita © 1969 Genjirou Mita
All rights reserved.

Translation by Mariko Shii Gharbi
English editing by Richard Stull

Published in the United States by:
MUSEYON INC.
1177 Avenue of the Americas, 5th Floor
New York, NY 10036

Museyon is a registered trademark.
Visit us online at www.museyon.com

Originally published in Japan in 1969 by POPLAR Publishing Co., Ltd.
English translation rights arranged with POPLAR Publishing Co., Ltd.

Printed in Shenzhen, Guangdong, China

ISBN 978-1-940842-03-5

0150401